# The Little Gray Bunny

Barbara Barbieri McGrath

*Illustrated by* Violet Kim

ini Charlesbridge

For Quinn with love
—B. B. M.

For my parents and
everyone who believes
in my art
—V. K.

Text copyright © 2013
by Barbara Barbieri McGrath
Illustrations copyright © 2013
by Violet Kim

Published by Charlesbridge
85 Main Street
Watertown, MA 02472
(617) 926-0329
www.charlesbridge.com

Library of Congress Cataloging-in-Publication Data
McGrath, Barbara Barbieri, 1954–
    The little gray bunny / Barbara Barbieri McGrath ;
illustrated by Violet Kim.
        p. cm.
    Summary: In this version of "The Little Red Hen," set
at a farm, the other animals eat and play while the little
gray bunny does all the chores in the barn, until one
day he teaches them a lesson about laziness.
    ISBN 978-1-58089-394-7 (reinforced for library)
    ISBN 978-1-58089-395-4 (softcover)
1. Folklore.  2. Rabbits—Folklore—Juvenile literature.
3. Animals—Folklore—Juvenile literature.  4. Laziness—
Folklore—Juvenile literature. [1. Folklore.]  I. Kim,
Violet, ill.  II. Little red hen. English.  III. Title.

PZ8.1.M176Lhp 2013
398.2—dc23   [E]   2012000788

Printed in China
(hc) 10 9 8 7 6 5 4 3 2 1
(sc) 10 9 8 7 6 5 4 3 2 1

Illustrations done in watercolor, pen, and gouache
Display type set in Kid Captain by Pink Broccoli Types
Text type set in Hunniwell by Aah Yes Fonts
Color separations by KHL Chroma Graphics, Singapore
Manufactured by Regent Publishing Services, Hong Kong
Printed September 2012 in Shenzhen, Guangdong, China
Production supervision by Brian G. Walker
Designed by Diane M. Earley

Once upon a time there was a lamb, a turtle, a duck, and a little gray bunny.

They all lived together in a cozy, comfy barn.

The lamb liked to nibble hay.

The turtle liked to play hide-and-seek
in the mirror.

The duck liked to float all day.

So the little gray bunny had to do
all the chores.

He wove the baskets,
baked the cupcakes,
and molded the jelly beans.

He mixed the bubble soap, stirred the dye,
weeded the tulip beds, and watered the lilies.

He groomed the goats, frightened the foxes, and prettied the pigs.

One day while he was checking the chickens,
he found hundreds of eggs in the pen.

"Goodness! This is my lucky day!" he said.

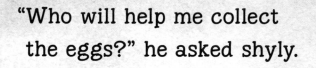

"Who will help me collect
the eggs?" he asked shyly.

"Not I," said the lamb.

"Not I," said the turtle.

"Not I," said the duck.

"Then I must do it myself,"
announced the little gray bunny.

"Who will help me gather wood to boil
the eggs?" asked the little gray bunny.

"Who, me?"
asked the lamb.

"Who's talking?"
asked the turtle.

"Does it involve drying
off?" asked the duck.

So each day the little gray bunny gathered
wood and boiled batches of eggs.

Soon clean, shiny eggs were piled
higher and higher outside the barn.

When all the eggs were dry and ready,
the little gray bunny wrinkled his nose and
pleaded, "Who will help me dye the eggs?"

"Is there hay?" asked the lamb.

"Did someone say something?"
asked the turtle.

"Do you even know me?"
asked the duck.

"These creatures have no artistic imagination," mumbled the little gray bunny.

After days of creating bright, beautiful eggs, the little gray bunny moaned, "Please, my friends, who will help me load these eggs into the wagon?"

"Baaaaaaaaaaa . . . humbug!" said the lamb.

"Who's out there?" said the turtle.

"Do eggs sink or float?" said the duck.

"I need to break this disturbing pattern,"
said the little gray bunny.

He gently placed the eggs in the wagon.

"Who will help me haul the eggs to hide in the hay meadow by the pond?" the little gray bunny asked.

"Hay, you say?" said the lamb.

"Hide, you say?" said the turtle.

"Pond, you say?" said the duck.

"EGGS-CELLENT!" exclaimed
the little gray bunny.

But the lamb, the turtle, and the duck just followed behind the wagon as the little gray bunny pulled the heavy eggs to the meadow.

"You are planning to help me hide the eggs, right?" he said with a sigh.

"I'm good,"
munched the lamb.

"Peek-a-boo!" said
the turtle.

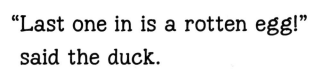

"Last one in is a rotten egg!"
said the duck.

The little gray bunny hid all the eggs.
When he was done, he announced, "Who
would like to go on an egg hunt? If you fill
your baskets, you will get a treat!"

"I would!" said the lamb.

"I would! A head start would
be appreciated!" said the turtle.

"Don't start without me!"
said the duck.

The three friends scurried around the field, hunting for eggs to put in their baskets.

When they couldn't carry any more,
they brought their baskets to the little
gray bunny. "Who wants a treat?"
asked the little gray bunny sweetly.

"I do!" said the lamb.

"I do!" said the turtle.

"I do!" said the duck.

"Well, well, well," said the little gray bunny. "I found the eggs. I boiled the eggs. I dyed the eggs. I hauled the eggs to the meadow, and I hid the eggs.

"And now I'm going to eat these jelly beans and cupcakes all by myself."

Then the little gray bunny winked
and said, "But here are your treats."

CRAAAACK!